THE MIDDLE GROUND

THE MIDDLE GROUND

ZOE WHITTALL

RAVEN BOOKS
an imprint of
ORCA BOOK PUBLISHERS

Library and Archives Canada Cataloguing in Publication

Whittall, Zoe
The middle ground / written by Zoe Whittall.
(Rapid reads)

ISBN 978-1-55469-288-0

I. Title. II. Series: Rapid reads
PS8595.H4975M53 2010   C813'.6   C2009-907249-1

First published in the United States, 2010
Library of Congress Control Number: 2009942223

Summary: Missy Turner's ordinary life is turned upside down
when she is taken hostage in a botched robbery at the local café,
and she finds herself questioning the validity of everything
she's always believed in.

Orca Book Publishers gratefully acknowledges the support for
its publishing programs provided by the following agencies: the
Government of Canada through the Canada Book Fund and the
Canada Council for the Arts, and the Province of British Columbia
through the BC Arts Council and the Book Publishing Tax Credit.

Design by Teresa Bubela
Cover photography by Getty Images

ORCA BOOK PUBLISHERS   ORCA BOOK PUBLISHERS
PO Box 5626, Stn. B   PO Box 468
Victoria, BC Canada   Custer, WA USA
V8R 6S4   98240-0468

www.orcabook.com
Printed and bound in Canada.

13 12 11 10 • 4 3 2 1

For my small-town girl

CHAPTER ONE

When he put the gun to my neck, I closed my eyes. A simple reflex. I imagined the cold metal tip was really just a magic marker, a wet cat's nose, or the small super-ball my son was always losing behind the couch cushions.

What happens when you feel the graze of a gun against your skin? Either you die or your whole life is changed.

I'd been doing this thing while drinking black coffee. I would close my eyes so I could pretend it still had cream in it. Apparently, you can lose five pounds in a month just by giving up the half-and-half. I'd been trying to psych myself out. Eyes shut, I'd imagine it all differently.

It didn't work with the gun either.

It could have been any ordinary day, really. It started out that way. I poured a cup of coffee into my favorite *We Can Make a Difference!* mug. I spooned a lump of cat food into a dish for Simon. Balancing both cup and dish, I kicked open the screen door. It was one of those beautiful summer days that promised perfect photographs. Idyllic after-work swims in the river.

"Siiii-mon!" The cat jumped from his oak-tree perch in the backyard. He waddled up, his one eye sparkling up at me.

I rescue stray cats. They come and go. But Simon has always stayed close. Ever since I found him. A tiny orange-and-white kitten hiding under our overturned canoe in the backyard, bleeding from his left eye.

That was thirteen years ago. I nursed him back to health, and he never left. Simon knows about loyalty.

Until that day, I thought I did too.

I stood on the chipped brown deck that Dale was always promising to restain and sipped my coffee. My bare feet were dirty and tanned. A white *V* from my flip-flops stared up at me. Next door, Lydia was sitting in her fold-out chair, having a morning cigarette before waking the kids. Like always.

I remember everything about that morning, though it was like so many others. Maybe that's why I do.

"Morning, Missy." She nodded, inhaling.

"Gonna be hot today, eh?" I'd answered back. What I was really thinking was, *Our houses are too close together*. That and, *She must have had her tits done*. Nipples don't point skyward like that after three kids are finished pawing at them. Her legs were shiny and perfectly tanned. She uses a fake oily color cream on them that I instinctively distrust. She tried to convince me to use it anyway. I tried it once. For two weeks my legs looked like someone colored on them with orange highlighter.

Still, there wasn't really much pretty about Lydia. Maybe from ten feet away she looked pretty. But up close, her features were awkwardly placed and covered in too much concealer.

We both stared out into our yards. I'd hoped she wouldn't want to talk. It was too early. Anyway, she really only liked to talk about herself. And she wasn't that interesting. In high school she was really geeky. She wore thick round glasses and played the trombone. She wasn't all that smart or anything, like some of the other nerdy kids. Then she went away to college. She came back all sex and confidence. Sometimes though, like when she smoked in the mornings, she still looked the picture of grade-nine awkwardness.

Behind our row of postwar bungalows and former farmhouses was what we used to call Conner's field. Now, two rows of identical pink brick duplexes filled the land between our street and the highway overpass. We used to live in a small town. Now the city stretched so far we were almost a suburb. The people in the pink houses took the train to the city to work and shopped at the new superstore on the edge of town.

Main Street, where I worked, was the same old stretch of stores. In many ways we were still a small town. People talked to each other. And everyone knew everyone else's business all the time. Like I knew all about Lydia's husband, who runs Jonny's Gas Bar. He cheated on her with a woman who moved to town and opened a yoga studio in her basement. To get back at him, Lydia slept with the gym teacher from the high school. That was Mr. Ronson, one of the fifty or so Ronsons in town. Now Jonny and Lydia are back to being "so in love." Or so Lydia exclaims any chance she gets. They spent a weekend at a couple's retreat in the mountains where they had to "concentrate on their essential oneness."

But I don't mind the gossip. Mostly because no one has ever had an excuse to talk about boring old Missy Turner anyway. Maybe in high school they did. When I got pregnant before graduation. But now, I'm just like everyone else.

I was never one of those girls prone to dreaming about getting away. Why leave somewhere quiet and comfortable? Where someone you love was always within arm's reach. Until that day, I thought I was pretty happy. My husband was mostly wonderful. Besides occasionally cutting his toenails in my presence, he wasn't half bad to have around.

Dale and I fell in love in the last year of high school. We both worked one of the concession booths at the fall fair. On a sugar high after too many green and pink slushies, we giggled into each other's arms. For our six-month anniversary, he took me to Lollapalooza. Six months used to be such a long time.

After Courtney Love's tearful elegy for her recently deceased husband, I lost my virginity in the parking lot. There's a photo of us standing outside the van afterward. Him wearing the red wool hat with the Beastie Boys patch on it. My hair bleached and puffy with little pink barrettes holding the mess back. I was wearing a plaid dress. Both of us were in combat boots. We look like babies in those photos but thought we were so tough, so old.

Eight months later Michael arrived. Early and so tiny, red and screaming. Despite all the pamphlets claiming my life was over, despite both of our parents urging me to give our son up for adoption, we opted for parenthood. It was probably the first instinctive thing I'd done in my life. And it worked out. Sometimes things do. For a while anyway.

When Mike was two, we tried living in the city for a year. Our apartment was one room on the sixteenth floor. I hated how the paint in the bathroom peeled, and the tap trickled constantly. And someone, somewhere, was always screaming. We were cramped. I worked at night in a café. Dale went to school during the day. We never saw each other. I don't think I've ever been so lonely, with only the company of a toddler.

When we came home after two semesters, we felt so broken. We came close to breaking up. Our families stepped in and helped out. Dale decided to get a job at the plant where his dad worked. We settled into my great-uncle's house after he went into a nursing home. At the end of our first summer, we no longer felt like we'd failed. We decided we'd just the made right choice. It sounds corny, or boring, but seriously, I feel lucky.

My parents live two miles away. We get together every Sunday. Our house is paid off. Michael is fifteen and he isn't making online hit-lists or doing meth or impregnating the girl down the block. He's smarter than we were as kids. He likes the outdoors. He plays guitar and watches lots of movies. Very normal. I think maybe he turned out so sweet because I *was* so young. I could still remember being a kid. I didn't talk to him like he was an idiot just because he was young. I read to him and made sure he knew he could be whoever he wanted to be. But for all my efforts, there was probably a lot of luck involved.

Mike was heading off to camp that day. Leaving home for the first time by himself. A wilderness adventure camp called Out of Bounds. According to the brochure, it was a place where teenagers *battle the wilderness and try to survive!* It promised to *build character* and *make lifelong friends*. Mike had been packing and repacking his oversized backpack for a week. Finally the day had arrived.

For weeks I'd been telling everyone how happy I was going to be to have the house to myself. I wasn't going to miss the sound of zombie-killing video games or the persistent stink of gym equipment. But you want to know the truth? I was feeling like a suck. One of those mothers who tear up thinking of her baby out in the world alone. My little wolf cub! I thought. I annoyed myself with those thoughts. Most of the time I still feel like I'm seventeen. Really. But somehow I'm thirty-three.

I've become one of those mothers I used to make fun of. I'm *my* mother. I understood her now. The way she used to cry when she dropped me off at the lake for two weeks of bible camp in the summers.

* * *

I'd decided to make a bowl of oatmeal for Michael. I dotted it with fresh blueberries. When I went downstairs to wake him, he was already up.

"I've been researching what to do if we encounter a bear," he said. In the cave of his basement bedroom, the only light emanated from the glow of his computer screen. Until he was thirteen his bedroom was upstairs beside ours. Suddenly he proclaimed it a baby's room. He decided he'd "have the whole downstairs now, please." We didn't really mind. For years it was supposed to be a sewing room for me and a workout area for Dale. Neither got much use.

Last summer Mike worked in the fields for six weeks corn-detasseling. Our area is big on agriculture, the unofficial corn capital of the country. He wised up this year with the camp. Applied in spring to be a counselor-in-training. Smart, my kid, avoiding the 5:00-AM wake-ups and the brutal heat of the fields. I know that eventually he's going to want to go away to university and live in the city. He's told me often that he can't wait to see the world.

"Well, it's good you're prepared," I mustered. "Now come up and eat your cereal."

Upstairs, he patted down his oatmeal with thick spoonfuls of brown sugar. I tried to pretend I was happy to have him out of my hair for six weeks. He picked all the blueberries out and dropped them on a pile of napkins.

"Pass the milk," he mumbled, like always.

"You nervous?"

"No way...whatever. It'll be fun." He looked nervous, oversized limbs shaking under the table. He picked up two berries and ate them.

"Eat some fresh fruit," I said, pushing half a banana and some apple slices toward him. "You'll probably be living on the dried stuff all summer." He took some slices to appease me.

Dale had said goodbye to him the night before, on his way out to a midnight shift at the plant. He was due home at eight thirty. I could go days without seeing him when he was on a night rotation. Just traces of toothpaste on the sink, socks in the hamper, dregs of coffee in a mug in the sink.

The last time we spoke, I could tell Dale was a little worried for Michael. Though he tried not to show it.

"I can't believe he's old enough to go off on his own," he said. "Do you ever think about the freedom we're going to have in a few years? It kind of blows my mind."

I was trying not to think about it much. Dale seemed excited. "We could travel! We could take that trip across the country like we always planned. I could turn the basement into a jam space, maybe get some recording equipment."

I wanted to get excited about it too, but I couldn't stop feeling sad whenever the future came up.

We packed up the car, and I dropped Mike off at the school parking lot. One of many parents embarrassing their kids with too-long hugs. "Mo-om." My name had become two syllables lately. "I'm not going off to Afghanistan."

Ever since our cousin James went off to Afghanistan, it was Mike's retort for everything. "Let me learn how to drive. I'm not going off to Afghanistan."

By the time I got to work, my tears had dried, and I told myself to buck up. Worst part of the day is over, I thought.

Not so.

* * *

For ten years I'd worked at Harlowe's Hardware, a family-owned business where I knew all the customers. I was known around town as Missy from the Hardware Store. Mr. Harlowe usually only came in on Saturdays to sign checks. I managed the staff and did the accounting. I kept the back office running and the customers happy. My favorite part of the job was teaching people how things worked. Especially women who had no idea how to hammer in a nail. I felt useful. I like working with my hands and understanding the mechanics of things.

That day, however, Mr. Harlowe was standing behind the counter when I got in.

No one else was there. Instead of greeting me with a grandfatherly hug and some terrible new joke, he avoided eye contact. His face looked apologetic.

"Missy," he said. "I'm afraid I have some bad news."

Laid off. It sounded so passive. Like someone gently pushing you onto the couch to reimagine your life in some other way.

It was happening a lot lately to people I knew. *The economy*, the newspapers said. People around here will always need hammers and nails, I'd thought. No one will ever stop needing to build things. I'm safe.

Not so.

I could see Mr.Harlowe's lips moving and I could hear the occasional series of words. "Selling to a developer" and "getting older, Mona's had the stroke, you know." "Happy to write you a stunning reference letter." "You're still young...Lots of options."

* * *

Then I was back in my car. I just sat there for a few minutes. Soaking in the shock. I resisted heading straight over to the corner store to buy cigarettes to smoke my brains out. I'd quit three months ago and had just started to find it repulsive. Instead, I drove to my sister's place. She runs a day care out of her home in an even smaller town just north of us.

It took three tries to get her to understand *I Lost My Job* with the screaming and crying of the Denver twins, who do everything, including throwing up and screaming, at the same time.

Jackie looked at me over the fuss and mess of four kids and shrugged. "Maybe this is your big chance to do something different with your life."

The girl twin threw up again. I cleaned up the mess while Jackie calmed her down and called the kids' mother.

"But I don't want another life. I like things the way they are."

"Everyone can see, Missy, you need some adventure. My god, try something new for once. Dale has a good job, it's not like you're gonna be homeless. When one door closes…"

"Oh, for god's sake, I wanted to get some support, not some kicky optimistic bullshit. I can't believe you're not being understanding. This is very upsetting!" My voice cracked. I couldn't believe how worked up I was feeling. A big change, and I had no control. I stole a cigarette from Jackie's pack on the table and left her with the screaming and crying.

I drove back into town on the road that winds along the river. I smoked half the cigarette before quitting again. The shops on Main Street suddenly seemed to have a different look to them. I parked in the lot behind Callie's Café, where I usually went for take-out on my lunch break. I went in through the back door and checked the bulletin board by the bathrooms for job ads. There were none. Just lost kittens and notices for the summer church picnic. I sat up front at the counter, where I assumed single people usually sit. I couldn't remember the last day I didn't have every moment planned.

As I opened up the newspaper that lay on the counter, I glanced at Harlowe's across the street. There was now a large CLOSED sign on the front door. Customers walked up, stopped and tried the door over and over, despite the sign.

The only other customers at Callie's at ten thirty in the morning were a couple of seniors in a back booth. The waitress, my youngest cousin Christina, brought me a cup of coffee and a menu. The place was sort of a hub in town. You could buy a sandwich, rent from an assortment of

DVDs behind the counter, or sit and read a newspaper all day in one of the burgundy booths that lined the perimeter. In one of them, *Led Zeppelin Rules* was carefully inked onto the tabletop. I swear it was there when I was four.

Christina moved a strand of her long black hair out of her eyes and handed me a spoon for my coffee. "You're looking a little rough, Missy. What's up?"

"I got laid off." It surprised me to say it.

"Oh man, that sucks." This was Christina's answer to most things. She used to be a beautiful girl until she started reading vampire novels. Now she has black hair with a blue streak. She dresses like Dracula and saves all her tips, intending to move to the city to find her vampire prince.

I scanned the classifieds. There were two notices. One for a forklift operator, another to be in medical studies. I turned back to the front page. The cover story was about the upcoming summer fair. Nothing ever happened in our town. It was a wonder we even had a newspaper.

"The trouble is, I don't know anything else I'd like to do."

I took two coffees to go, thinking Dale would want one before he went to bed around eleven. He was one of those people who could drink six cups a day and still sleep like a baby. Perhaps, I thought, I could turn the day around with morning sex and a little afternoon gardening. After all, there was no risk of Mike coming home.

Sounded blissful, actually. Perhaps we could have another kid, and I could be a stay-at-home mom for a few years. Or I could start my own business—catering, or a line of natural soaps. The possibilities are really endless. Maybe Jackie is right, and I just have to calm down a bit to realize it. By the time I pulled into the driveway, my brain was positively on fire with the possibilities of my new life. I wanted to run through the front door and grab Dale, energize him with all the ideas I had for us.

But when I turned my key in the door, my gut sensed something was off. Things in the house didn't look the same. I could hear voices in the kitchen. I thought perhaps it was the oddity of being home on a weekday or the lack of Mike's presence. But when I walked into the kitchen from the living room, holding my tray of coffees, I couldn't have been more surprised if I'd found a family of aliens sitting at the table.

I dropped the coffees on the floor.

CHAPTER TWO

I don't really remember driving back into town. About twenty minutes later, I found myself back in the parking lot behind Callie's Café. Mouth dry and heart still up-tempo. My right shoe soaking with hot creamy coffee. I suppose I'd wanted to go back in time and just not know. Just stay at the café instead of leaving. I placed my forehead on the wheel and sobbed.

Eventually, I stopped crying and managed to get my breathing back close to normal. I wiped my nose on a napkin from the glove compartment stash. The sun was shining brightly, just a hint of cloud on the horizon. I watched people walking about, doing their errands, walking into the post office across the street from the parking lot. Everyone had somewhere to be at this time of day.

I felt like I was watching a movie. People all looked strange to me. Though, of course, I recognized almost everyone. I got out of the car. I walked around to the front door and went back inside to sit at the counter. There were no other customers. I tried to pretend everything was normal.

The room looked too bright and seemed blurred at the edges. Christina raised her eyebrows at me. I noticed her brow piercing was scabbed and gross. "Back so soon?"

"Hungry," I muttered. "And I dropped my coffee."

"You look wrecked. I guess you're really taking this job thing hard, eh?"

"I suppose."

"It's just a job, right? You'll get another one." Christina bit her nails and shrugged. Oh, how I longed to be Christina's age. When jobs were things that came and went. And boyfriends weren't husbands. I remember her toddling down the aisle at our wedding, the meandering little flower girl.

"How are you doing, Christina?"

"Cook keeps calling in sick. I gotta make the food too, so I'm pretty bummed."

I ordered one of the pre-made egg-salad sandwiches they kept in a case beside the donuts and another coffee. I pretended to read so I could shield my tears behind the thin inky newspaper. The sandwich looked as appetizing as a pile of dirt. I peeled the crust off of one side. Christina settled into her book on the stool beside the counter. I thought about calling my mother, but I didn't want to upset her. I was still too mad at Jackie to try her. I just wanted to crawl into a hole, figure things out on my own.

When I heard the door open and the bell's chime, I expected to see one of the seniors hobbling in for coffee. Instead, it was a tall man in a red plaid hunting jacket, a cap pulled over his eyes. He had broad shoulders and looked a bit like Jude Law. A man's body, his face unshaven for a day or two, but still boyish.

He walked up to Christina at the counter, her face buried behind a hardcover library book called *Vanity's Angels*. He coughed. She looked up.

"Uh, coffee to go. Black."

"Can you believe her?" I ask him, pointing at the latest celebrity teen dream photographed with a baby on one knee, driving recklessly through LA. My hand shook against the newspaper. I probably looked crazy. I certainly felt crazy. Every time I closed my eyes, I saw the scene that had just unfolded in my kitchen. My own freaking kitchen.

"Yeah, she's crazy," he said, smiling sideways at me, then looked down. He tapped his fingers on the counter. "My kid loves her music though."

Christina fussed with the coffee pot and turned back. "Sorry, I have to make a fresh pot. I forgot to turn the warming burner on and this one isn't hot anymore. Sorry." She didn't really look sorry at all.

She turned and wandered over to the cupboards behind the counter, fussing with a shiny gold bag of coffee grounds. She emptied them into the machine and pressed the start button. Then she sat back on her tall stool and picked up her book again.

The man smelled so good, like woodchips and some kind of sweet soap. He tapped his foot anxiously. A drop of sweat from his brow fell onto the white countertop. I was staring. God, stop that, I told myself.

I turned back to the paper. I was trying to figure out what to do. Should I go home?

All I wanted to do was punch something. Or scream. Feel anything but the rotating bursts of shock.

Another drop of sweat dripped onto the counter.

"Oh my god!" yelped Christina.

I looked up. The man was leaning over the counter, one hand grasping the over-sized rosary Christina wore around her neck. The other held a gun to her chest.

"Empty the register and I won't shoot, please, miss. I don't want to hurt anyone," he said very clearly, using the same tone of voice you might use to say, *I'd also like a piece of pie.*

CHAPTER THREE

I nstead of quietly backing toward the door or trying to dial 9-1-1 on my cell phone—I kept it turned off and buried under all my purse crap—I walked around the counter and stood beside Christina. Maybe it was the look of complete terror on her face. Or the fact that I had held her as a squirming pink newborn. Or the whimper she made as she dropped the book and fumbled with the cash register.

He let go of her necklace and placed both hands on the small pistol.

"Don't hurt her," I heard myself saying. "She's just a girl. Whole life ahead of her."

"Shut up, lady, and get back around to this side of the counter, all right? Don't push any buttons. Just give me the money, and I'll be on my way." He tapped his foot, like he was impatiently waiting at the bank on any non-felony errand.

The scene was nothing like on TV, where the music starts, cueing your heart to speed up. It felt slow, like molasses pouring from a cup. Christina handed him a handful of bills. He stuffed them into a yellow bag advertising the new superstore on the outskirts of town. It couldn't have been more than a hundred bucks.

What you should know about our town is that we never usually see the cops. Our firemen are volunteers. It's faster to drive yourself to the hospital than wait for an ambulance to arrive from almost an hour away. The local police station was on the edge of town near the mall. Sometimes the state police stopped speeders on the highway, but generally we didn't have much need for cops. Nothing ever happened. People were mostly nice and looked out for each other. The worst we got were teen-agers joyriding or an occasional fistfight after the one bar closed. But even these were rare.

But for some reason, that day—and just at that moment—Jerry Ronson parked the precinct's lone cruiser in front of Callie's. Jerry used to beat the crap out of my older brother in high school. He'd parlayed his schoolyard bullying into a job with the local force. I don't hate a lot of people, but I pretty much hate Jerry. Besides bullying my brother, he also tried to date-rape my sister at the prom. He still has a scar on the side of his face from a bottle she'd smashed into it. She never called the cops. They just avoided each other for a few weeks until my sister left town for college. When she came back, they continued to avoid each other as adults. Even his uniform bugged me. That and the fact he was now respected just because he could complete six weeks of boot camp and a few community college courses.

Through the giant window that read *Callie's Coffee & Pie!*, we watched as he opened the door to his cruiser. Old Mrs. Jackson walked up to him, and they began to chat.

When I saw Jerry, I didn't think, Thank god, we're saved. I knew in my gut that Jerry versus this guy was going to mean bad things. Confrontation. Christina whimpered again.

"Fucking cop," the man swore. "Jesus Christ! No one say anything, I mean it!"

There were just us three in the whole café.

He started mumbling, "What am I going to do? This was supposed to be easier.

I swear, if that cop comes in, I will shoot everyone. I swear! My car is out front. What the fuck am I going to do? I didn't think this through."

I looked at Christina, her eyes were pleading. "Christina, go outside and tell Jerry you need to ask him a question about something for school. Tell him you want to be a cop. Keep him occupied. Then"—I turned to the robber and looked him in the eye—"you can go out the back door."

I motioned toward the door I'd come through earlier that morning. It had a faded *Live Bait Out Back* sign on it. A drawing of a smiling worm on a hook. They hadn't sold bait in years. The pulp and paper mill ten miles upstream made sure the fish weren't very appetizing. No one moved.

I used a voice I normally reserved for toddlers. "Put the gun on me. Let Christina go outside. She won't tell him. Right, Christina? Or *He. Will. Hurt. Me.*" I looked at her, trying my best to convince her I was actually being serious.

Christina nodded. "Yes, okay."

"He'll let me go, and I'll come outside and we'll all pretend that nothing happened. Okay? It's just money, not worth getting killed over."

The robber pulled the gun away from Christina and pointed it toward me.

"After all, if justice doesn't find you now, it will catch up with you later."

He ignored my conjecture.

"Come around here," he ordered. I raised my hands in the air.

"Why? Just run. Go. I won't say anything. I promise."

"I'm the one with the gun, missy."

I laughed. I laugh when I'm nervous. I got the giggles at my grandfather's funeral.

"What?"

"Nothing. My name is Missy, is all. What's yours?"

"This isn't a party, lady. Come around the counter. NOW."

I walked around the counter, worried that at any moment I might stream pee onto the tiled floor. He put one arm around my shoulder and the gun to my neck.

"Go, Christina," I said, as sternly as I could under the circumstances.

Christina toddled toward the door in her pointy heels.

He watched her through the window. Then he backed away and pulled me with him. "Turn around."

I did as he said, and he put the gun at my back. We walked out the back door. This wasn't in my plan.

"Just run!" I said. "You don't have to take me with you. I won't say anything."

"You'll run right out there to the cop," he said, "and that can't happen."

"No, I won't. I hate that cop. I won't help make him a hero, that's for sure."

We stood next to the dumpsters in the parking lot where I'd parked my car. He took in what I said. "Yeah, I hate cops too." As if we were just swapping opinions.

"I didn't say I hate cops; I said I hate *that* cop."

He put his arm around my neck again, gun at my side. Like we were slow dancing and had stopped moving in the middle of a turn. He seemed confused.

"Now is your chance to escape," I said. I thought he'd blindly follow orders.

But he kept the gun on me, his sweaty arm chafing my neck. I started to feel like I might be breathing my last breath. This could be it—this terrible, fucking horrifying day. Mike won't even know, out in the woods for six weeks. Dale will find this guy and shoot him and spend the rest of his life in jail. Mike will be orphaned. My mother crying on the evening news, holding up a photo of me from our wedding.

"What do you *want*? Run! Get away! Leave me alone. I won't say anything." He turned me around, gently pushing me back against the ice machine. Face to face, I considered my options. Could I kick him? Thirty-three, I thought. I'm only thirty-three. Earlier I'd felt too old to start over. Now I suddenly felt so young. So inexperienced.

"My car," he stuttered. "I need to drive! I can't go out front and just waltz by the cop into my car." He put the gun at his side and stepped back. "And I don't want to go to jail," he whimpered. "You need to help me. I have kids!"

I looked up at him. He looked like a scared kid himself. "You don't understand," he muttered. "I had no choice. Everyone keeps fucking with me. I have the *worst* luck."

In that moment, I probably could have turned around and run back into the café and yelled for help. It was something about the way he looked at me. That and the fact that everything that had once mattered in my life had disappeared in the last four hours or so.

Instead I reached into my pocket and handed him my car keys.

"What the hell…white KIA, over there."

"You're giving me your car?" He said this the same way he might have asked, *Is that really a giant pink elephant?*

"Yes, just fucking take it!"

"Okay, okay, thanks. I owe you something big." He looked at me, and his features softened. He was really handsome. I blushed.

I nodded, my hands still up in the air defensively. "Yes, you do. So don't fuck with that. You owe me."

He threw me his keys. "It's the red four-door out in front of the hardware store. Leave it in the Walmart parking lot at Sunnytown Mall tonight around eight. I'll leave yours by the McDonald's entrance.

If you tell the cops, I will find you and hurt you and your family. Mark my words."

"That's a nice way to pay back a favor."

"I'm sorry, but I have to. I can't get caught."

"I promise. I won't say a word."

He backed away, his eyes on mine. "Is your name really Missy?"

"Yup."

"You're beautiful, Missy."

He ran to my car and got in awkwardly. The seat was too far forward for his long limbs. I watched him drive off, turning left away from downtown and peeling away. I leaned against the ice machine. I looked at his keys. They were on a square metal keychain that said *Death Before Dishonor*. I buried them in my skirt pocket.

I turned and tried to go back inside the café. My hands were shaking so much that at first I couldn't turn the doorknob. When the door finally opened, Christina and Jerry were rushing in through the front door, weaving through the tables toward me.

"Where is he?" Christina asked, her voice trembling with emotion. "I finally told him, Missy. I had to. When you didn't come outside right away, I was so scared! I thought he'd kidnapped you! I thought maybe the cops could save you."

"You did the right thing," Jerry said. He then spoke briefly into the two-way radio he pulled off his belt. He looked excited, like he was almost happy something like this had happened.

"I need you to tell me everything," he said. It was then that I made a decision that surprised me most of all.

"He ran off on foot," I said, "down Mercer Street."

CHAPTER FOUR

When they turned the TV cameras on, I lost the ability to speak. This is funny, because I can talk to anyone, anytime. I am the furthest thing from shy.

It's like my teeth turned to sand, and I couldn't say a thing. The light blinded me and I squinted. The girl from the TV news looked aggravated but smiled with all her teeth. "Just relax. Just tell us what happened." Her perfume was overpowering. It made my stomach turn.

Christina, who was all jumpy beside me, dropped her smoke on the sidewalk and squished it with her heel.

"It was crazy!" she said. "He was real mean. He pointed the gun right at me. And my cousin here, Missy, she's a real hero. She got him to calm down, right? She's the reason we're not all dead right now. True story."

"What did the assailant look like?"

"He was huge," Christina said, "like a logger. Big arms. I bet he's already been to prison 'cause he had tattoos on his hands."

It was at that moment that I realized the robber would probably see this footage, possibly in some terrible highway-side motel. And he'd come after me for telling.

"How does it feel to be a hero, Mrs. Turner?"

"Oh, well, I'd only be a hero if I'd have caught him, right?"

"But you may have saved the day, anyhow?"

"I suppose."

She turned back to the camera. "A quiet, peaceful town rocked today by a brazen midmorning holdup, and"—she paused dramatically—"the gunman is still at large. He fled on foot and may not have had a getaway car. Drivers in the area are advised not to pick up hitchhikers and to take special care of their children walking home from school. He is described as white, mid-thirties, with tattooed hands. More details at six o'clock. Back to you, James." She stood still a few moments longer, until the camera shut off.

"That it?" she asked a man with a cell phone.

"Yup."

"Great. Let's get the hell out of this shit-hole." I suppose she didn't realize I was still standing there next to the bright yellow sign advertising *Coffee and a Fresh Muffin— $1.79!!* "This town gives me the creeps."

She reached down to fix the clasp on her shoe and noticed me.

"Sorry," she muttered, "I've had a bad day."

She got back into the big black Hummer with the news station name on the side before I could say, "*You've* had a bad day?"

I was calmed by her telling the public he was on foot. That way he'd know that I wasn't a liar. I'd be safe. I pictured him in my car, the insurance papers in the glove box. He'd know my address. He'd see the paperbacks borrowed from the library down the block. He could piece me together. I can't believe I gave a criminal my car. Would my insurance count that as stolen? I certainly didn't feel like I really had a choice. It was the only way I could think to get him to leave.

At the police station Christina and I drank the warm diet pop they offered us and gave our official statements. First we wrote down what happened in our own words. Then we answered their questions.

"Why didn't you just tell Jerry right away about the holdup?"

"Like I said, he said he was going to shoot everyone if Jerry came inside. Missy came up with a plan to let him get away without it becoming a hostage situation, right?"

"I decided," I jumped in, "that it was better to let him run off with the hundred bucks or whatever than try to catch him and wind up getting us all killed." The cop looked unimpressed.

"Why did you eventually decide to tell Jerry, Christina?"

I was sweating so hard I felt like they could tell right away that I was lying. I was part of it all. But what I was doing still made sense in some weird way. To protect us.

"Because Missy said she'd come right out after he got away, and she was taking so long I thought maybe he was hurting her."

"He wasn't going to just let me go—"

"Of course not," Jerry interrupted, like I was a total idiot.

I glared at him. I bet he's never had to deal with anything like this before. I kept explaining, "...like I expected him too. He didn't seem like he wanted to hurt anyone. He was just desperate. I thought, given the option, he'd run away. But he was confused, he thought I would tell."

"The police are trained in these kinds of situations. Did you ever think that maybe you shouldn't have taken the law into your own hands?" I had this vision of Jerry walking lazily into Callie's. He'd be taken completely off guard and shot in the chest before he even knew what was happening. And then the robber would have had to shoot Christina and me before he ran out. It could've gone that way. I explained the possibility.

"You watch too much TV, Mrs. Turner. It's a long way from robbery to mass murder."

I shrugged. "Maybe my quick thinking saved you." I couldn't help but egg him on. "He seemed desperate. He said that was what he would have to do. He did have the means, after all."

"You said he was polite, but then he threatened to take you all out? Which one was it? Was he a *nice* robber or a potential mass murderer?"

I swallowed hard, cheeks burning. "I guess he was a mix of both." Jerry looked down and made a mark on his paper. "I mean, he was crazy. Obviously, right? Criminals aren't exactly known for being predictable." Jerry stood up, and the other cop continued asking questions.

"I'm sorry, Mrs. Turner. I understand this was a traumatic experience for you." He looked back at Jerry to make a point.

I didn't believe the whole good-cop–bad-cop thing was actually a *thing*. "Was there anything distinctive about the way he looked? A scar, a tattoo?"

He had reddish blond hair and one black hoop earring. The kind you get at specialty piercing shops that stretch out your lobes. When he loosened his lumberjack jacket, I noticed he was wearing a *Corrosion of Conformity* T-shirt. I would have been the only one to see these things. In my periphery, I saw Jerry strutting around the office with older state police officers, looking like the pride of the county.

"No," I lied. "It all happened so fast. And he had the hat over his eyes. The tattoos on his hands, they were clovers, I think."

"No," Christina interrupted, "I think they were letters."

Truth is, there was one red heart, but that was it. It was all fading so fast. I just wanted him to get away and start over. I'm not certain why. He'd scared the shit out of me and I was angry. But mostly I felt adrenaline surge through my body and heard his desperate childlike voice exclaiming, "I have kids!"

When I tried to understand what I was feeling in that moment, it felt closest to sympathy. *Sympathy?* It made no sense.

I could have helped them solve the crime right there, but I didn't. I held the secret in my pocket. They could run the plates on his car and find his name. Search it for clues. But I knew the new, bizarre, alien version of me wanted to be the only one who knew. Wanted to take the car to him and try to figure out what would make someone pull out a gun to solve his problems. And I didn't want to hand it all to Jerry like a gift.

After all, they could scrutinize all the cars on the street and figure it out. If they did,

I would simply bury the keys in my garden and be done with it.

At the time, my plan seemed simple. In retrospect, I long to be able to go back and make different choices.

When I left the interrogation room and went into the lobby of the police station, Dale was standing there. "Missy! Jerry called me! Are you okay?" His eyes were pleading with me.

I looked right at him but didn't answer.

"Don't come home," I said eventually.

I turned to Judy, the female cop who had promised to take me home. I'd said I was too anxious to drive. I didn't bother to mention that my car was currently being driven by a maniac.

"I'll take that ride now," I said. I walked right passed Dale and down the steps. I waited next to the cruiser out front.

Judy was new in town. She had frizzy red hair and was from New Jersey. I found myself nervously chattering, pointing out all the places she might not know about yet. Like the best place to get pizza, and the story of the Carmichael triplets who still lived together above the old department store. The weird way they never made eye contact with anyone. Judy's husband was a painter. They wanted a quieter life and were drawn to the pace here, the inspiring scenery. They had recently bought a farm out near my sister's place. I nodded.

"How come you didn't go home with your husband?"

"Let's just say, I'm so mad at him I'm afraid I'll haul off and hit him."

Judy remained expressionless as she pulled up in front of my house. I thanked her for the ride. She nodded.

If this were a normal day, Dale would be waking up at four o'clock, the automatic coffeemaker already on.

The house was so empty and quiet.

The house next door was also empty. No one was home during the day on our street except Mrs. McGiven across the street. I felt like I was a spy on my own life. I looked into the living room, to the left when you walk in the front door. On the right was a cubby for boots and coats and the door out to the garage. You walk straight through to the dining room and turn left into the kitchen. It was small. We always talked about taking out the wall between the kitchen and dining room but never figured out what we'd do with the stove that was on that wall. Off the kitchen were the stairs that lead both downstairs to the basement and up to our bedroom and Mike's old room, now a guest room.

Simon brushed up against my leg. The robber's car keys weighed heavily in my pocket. I went downstairs to Mike's room. I stripped his bedding and put his sheets in the wash, along with the pile of dirty

T-shirts thrown in the corner. His room seemed so empty. I hadn't had access to it in years, not like this. Even while he was at school and I happened to be home, I'd only glance in and occasionally retrieve a moldy cup or plate. I never wanted to be one of those mothers who snooped. It was odd to have the time to look at all his objects, everything he thought was important.

I felt the weight of him being gone all summer. Then it dawned on me that this was only the beginning. One day he'd be gone for good. And perhaps I'd be single again. I'd have a whole new future, without the men I'd loved for fifteen years.

I dusted off his dresser, bottles of deodorant spray, a baseball trophy, a small comb. I wiped down his bookshelves, rows of science fiction, sports biographies, wilderness guides and horror paperbacks. A few true-crime books that used to belong to Dale. I picked up a biography of a cult leader who killed all his followers before the FBI moved in. In puffy red letters on the back, *What Makes a Man So Evil?* I tucked it under my arm and went back upstairs.

I tried to pretend everything was normal. But one moment I'd see the scene in the kitchen that I'd stumbled into that morning, the next I'd feel the gun on my neck. The house didn't feel my own anymore. The walls made me anxious. The sound of the clock ticking loomed. Outside, a car backfired, and my skin was instantly covered in sweat.

I'd rarely felt the house so empty without Mike and Dale. I normally relished the rare opportunity to be alone, but the quiet was unnerving. I kept seeing Christina yelp and drop her book. I felt the pressure of the robber's arm against my neck.

I heated up some leftover pasta but couldn't eat it. I didn't want to be alone but couldn't bear the thought of calling anyone either. The phone rang and rang, and the answering machine filled with messages from nosy neighbors and Mr. Harlowe and Jackie and my mom. Everyone who had heard about what happened. I turned on the TV but only paced in front of it, until the coverage of the robbery came on. It was a very short clip, mostly Christina, with me standing beside her like a goofy, useless tree. Is that what I really look like now? So old. I used to be stylish and young. How did I start dressing like a mother who had given up?

The keys in my pocket continued to weigh me down. The obligation to drive his car. This *criminal's* car. I knew once I got in and turned the key, I was no longer a victim, but an accomplice. It made me want to throw up. Ever since I could first understand the messages in *Sesame Street* episodes as a child, I'd always felt I could determine right from wrong. This middle ground, it was new.

I considered calling the police station and explaining everything. Confessing. There was relief in that option, certainly. But also fear. And pity. What if this guy made a mistake in judgment, out of desperation? Certainly I could have compassion.

Finally, around eight in the evening, I took Mike's ten-speed out of the garage and adjusted the seat. I rode along the river and into town, like I was getting some exercise after dinner. Just like the gaggle of families walking in pairs, or the super athletic bicycle enthusiasts, zipping by me in their matching helmets.

Inside I was starting to feel like a criminal. Nothing like Missy Turner, hard-working, chatty, everyone's good friend and helpful neighbor.

It didn't feel terrible. It felt exciting.

CHAPTER FIVE

By dinnertime Main Street was pretty much empty. Only Jonny's Gas Bar and the tavern across the street were still open. Callie's was a full block away and closed at six. Every other business on the block shut by five. I had decided on the ride in that I would simply walk up to the car as though it were my own. I'd lock Mike's bike to a pole in the alley beside Callie's and come back for it in the morning. If anyone saw me, I would say it was my sister Jane's car. The one from the city who only comes home once a year. I'd invent an errand she'd sent me on.

My plan went smoothly. When I got in the car, I paused briefly to look around. I don't know what I expected to find, maybe drugs or a stash of weapons. A girl tied up in the trunk? I laughed out loud nervously.

Who was this man? In my head, I'd started calling him Red, for his hair, and the red jacket. His anger.

Even though it was hot out, I wore my thin black driving gloves. Just in case the car got fingerprinted later on. A distinctly real possibility, I thought. In the backseat was a car seat and several squished juice boxes. A rabbit's foot hung from the rearview mirror. In the glove box was a photo album trimmed in bright green fun fur and the insurance documents encased in a plastic folder. I picked up the photo album first. Inside were pictures of Red and his kids. Around a Christmas tree, at the beach, playing on the swings in a park. The insurance papers identified the robber. Roger MacMillan.

Age thirty-six. 345 Miller Street, Philadelphia. A long way from here. What was he doing in my little town?

He seemed like such an ordinary guy, not hiding anything. The car seat in the back was comforting. I am doing the right thing.

I drove out of town on Route 16 and veered onto the expressway. I started to feel almost comfortable. I could be anyone on this highway. I drove with purpose for five miles. That's what I'd liked about working at Harlowe's—every day I had tasks to fulfill. I was good at them; the focus drove me.

When I pulled into the Walmart parking lot, it was pretty full for a weeknight. But magically there were two spaces next to the McDonald's entrance. I got out my cell phone and turned it on. In the bottom of my purse I found the canister of pepper spray Dale got me for when I closed the store on Thursday nights. Not because anyone had ever hassled me or was likely to, but because Dale watched too much *CSI*.

I was early, so I turned on the radio. I sang along nervously, as though anyone could hear me outside the car. The autodial was mostly set to all-news radio stations, with one country and one classic rock. I watched people push their carts in and out of the store. Tired parents, excited children, people I could easily be.

I imagined what Red might be doing. I wondered if he was feeling nervous. I went over the vulnerable points on a man's body and tried to remember what I'd learned in a self-defense course so many years ago.

Then I scribbled a note to him and stuck it to the dashboard using a bit of chewing gum. It read: *I promised not to tell anyone, and I didn't. I'm waiting in the Walmart McDonald's, if you want to talk. Things happen for a reason. 812-555-8765. M.*

A few minutes later I saw my car drive up and park in a spot across from me. Red emerged with a small child in tow, a girl of about four. She had long black hair, uncombed, and wore a *Dora the Explorer* T-shirt. In her arms she held a little brown puppy about the size of a rabbit.

I got out of the car and smoothed the skirt of my red dress, one I hadn't worn since our tenth anniversary. It had embroidered cherries on the hem and a scoop neck. When I left the house it had made me feel confident. Biking along the river, I'd felt like a postcard of the kind of girl I'd never been. Now I just felt sweaty and overly bright in the already too-bright parking lot.

I nodded at Red—Roger—and said hello to his little girl. "Here are your keys, Roger," I said. We stood across from each other, as though we were both in the receiving line at a wedding. Oddly formal, like a version of ourselves we played out at a job interview.

He didn't seem surprised that I knew his name.

He handed me my keys, hanging from the mini-level keychain we sold at Harlowe's. His hands shook a little. "That's a nice puppy," I said to the girl, who looked me up and down silently.

After perhaps ten seconds she said, "His name is Strawberry Fields, and he has special powers."

"Wow," I said. "What powers?"

"He can see into the future," she said, shrugging.

Roger pulled out a pack of cigarettes. He took one and offered me the pack. I took one and handed them back. He lit mine with a silver Zippo, then his own. We stood for a moment, smoking.

"But he can't tell me what's in the future because he doesn't know English."

"Maybe you could learn how to speak dog," I offered.

She thought about this. "Yes, that is a good idea."

"Well, we better be going," said Roger, throwing down his half-smoked cigarette and stubbing it out with his boot. "Thanks for doing me that favor."

He opened the back door for his daughter and strapped her into the car seat. The puppy curled up on the floor below her. As he walked around to the driver's seat he said, "Have a good night, Missy Turner."

He drove off. I stood there and finished my cigarette. Then I walked to the curb and sat down in front of the line of stacked shopping carts. I burst into tears. Of relief, I suppose…relief that I had my car back and that a swarm of cops hadn't descended upon me.

I hadn't cried that much in years.

Finally I went into McDonald's and ordered a cup of terrible coffee. I sat down and pretended, for the second time that day, to read a newspaper. My phone rang and rang. Dale calling repeatedly, my mother, Jackie. Over and over, leaving concerned messages. Normal Missy, pre-today Missy, would have felt terrible guilt and returned all the calls immediately. Normal Missy would now be making egg-salad sandwiches on whole-wheat bread for Dale's lunch. Preparing to watch her regular Wednesday night TV shows. Her most pressing contemplation being whether or not to make a hair appointment or sign up for another yoga class.

I felt no guilt. They could all just relax. If they wanted to know what happened at Callie's, they could watch the news. I was feeling so done with it all.

Done.

After two hours Roger didn't show. The staff at McDonald's swept and mopped around me, eventually an overly cheerful Anna, according to her nametag, ushered me out the door.

By this point I was feeling foolish for suggesting the meet-up. Like one of those desperate women on Oprah who write criminals, hoping to snag a boyfriend. I could hear the voice of Judge Judy squawking at me in her shrill superior tone: "You trusted a criminal?"

I decided to call Jackie and confess everything. But when I got into the car, clicking on the wipers to clear away the sudden torrent of rain, on my dashboard was a note.

Dear Missy,

I'm so sorry for scaring you, and for threatening your family. Know that I would never really have hurt you, someone so beautiful and obviously loyal. I just needed the money, and I didn't want to go to jail. I know, these are sorry excuses, but I have become a weak man. I know now, after having watched you be so brave, that I will change. I have to change. I would like the opportunity to tell you I'm sorry in person. If you would like this, meet me at Johnson's Steakhouse just at the junction of Highway 12, tomorrow at ten a.m. I'll be in one of the back booths. My daughter will be back with my mother by then, so we can talk.

I folded up the paper. I put my phone away and decided to wait to tell Jackie everything.

CHAPTER SIX

When I pulled up in front of the house, it was dark. I found the living room covered in my favorite flowers: daisies, sunflowers and roses. In the middle of the kitchen table was a letter from Dale, in his impossible-to-understand scribble. I crumpled it up and stuffed it in my purse. I was relieved to see that he cared, that he was trying. But I was still too mad to read it. The answering machine was blinking endlessly on the counter. Fourteen messages, mostly from Dale, my mother and my sister. Where was I? Why wasn't

I picking up my cell? But there were also a couple asking for radio interviews, one from a newspaper journalist requesting a quote, and one from someone "checking facts and spellings." Finally there was one from Julia, a worker from County Victim and Witness Services. If I needed any advice or support, I could call her. Hadn't anything else newsworthy happened yet? I erased them all.

I gathered up all the flowers into an oversized clear garbage bag and put it in front of the door so Dale would trip on it in the morning.

I couldn't face our bedroom, so I crept downstairs into Mike's room. Mike, who had no idea his family was imploding as he hiked through the wilderness.

I turned on his computer and logged into my Facebook account, something I'd used to keep in touch with friends from high school who had moved away. I loved it for a while, seeing everyone's baby photos and the details of their lives. Then it got to be a pain. Like a party you can't just leave when you're bored. In the search box, I typed Roger's full name. He didn't seem like the type, but you never know, right?

I was a bit surprised when his profile popped up almost immediately. It turned out he lived not too far away. His photo was a bit blurry, a distant shot of someone who could be him walking with a German shepherd. Unlike a lot of my friends, he didn't keep his profile private.

He listed his likes as hair metal, Nirvana and old-school metal and punk. This made sense with the punk rock T-shirt he'd been wearing. Also skateboarding, tattoos, horses and dogs. His favorite movie was *Bandits* (the irony!). His favorite quote: "Be the Type of Person Your Dog Thinks You Are" and "Death Before Dishonor." That clinched it. All of his wall postings were out of date, but about six months previously there were a rash of postings from some of his forty-seven friends.

Man, I'm so sorry for your loss.

Call me if you need anything, or need us to take care of Trisha for a while.

We're here for you.

I love you, Rog. You can count on us during this difficult time.

I hope that fucker fries.

It appeared Roger hadn't logged in for about six months, after something major went down. It had me so curious. And so much more sympathetic.

I went upstairs and packed up a small bag with pajamas, a cosmetics case and an outfit for the morning. I stripped the bed and put the sheets in the wash, knowing this would confound Dale and he'd end up sleeping on a bare mattress and be pissed off. I picked up the phone to call Jackie while I organized.

"Hey, what a perfect time to finally call me back…at one in the freaking morning."

"I'm sorry, Jacks. I have to stay at your place, okay? I can't be here."

"I know. Mom told me."

"How the fuck does Mom know?"

"You know she's all-knowing."

"Dale must have called her. Can't I have even a bit of privacy?"

"She thinks you should—"

"I didn't ask for your opinions."

"Well, whatever. I'll go open the back door and pull out the couch in the basement. Stay as long as you want. Make the dirtbag suffer."

Since Jackie's first experience with a boy was the attack by Jerry, she had never developed any patience for men. Her husband was meek and did everything she said. He wouldn't even kill a spider.

Once at Jackie's, I curled up under an orange afghan and stared at the rows of

track-and-field trophies from her youth.
A photo from our wedding day in a bronze
frame was on the wall. I pulled it from its
nail and put it face down on top of some
old VHS tapes.

I only slept for maybe two hours. I kept
thinking of Dale, a confusing mix of anger,
hurt and loneliness. It made me even madder
that I felt this need for him, even though I
was so angry. I can't even be angry right!

I woke early and showered in the downstairs stall. I put on my other good dress.
A short black number Jackie helped me
pick out years ago. She had taken me with
her to the city for an art opening. Back
when she was still trying to make a go of
her sculptor career.

In the dim bathroom mirror I applied
eye shadow and some cover-up over the
slight bruise that had appeared on my
neck. The memory of that violence turned
my stomach, but, I reasoned, he didn't

know me then. He was desperate. Who knows what I'd do if I were ever desperate like that.

I matched the dress with a pair of Jackie's heeled boots from the alcove.

"Going job hunting," I mumbled to Jackie as she struggled to feed one of her early day-care kids at the kitchen table.

"Good luck," she said.

When I got in the car, I felt the thrill of having a secret and knowing that Dale was likely worried. My anger still surged, and I wanted him to wonder. I wanted to make him worry. I wanted him to understand that maybe his wife wouldn't wait around for him this time.

CHAPTER SEVEN

The diner was the kind of place my father would've secretly taken us kids to when we were young. My mother would've thought it was trashy. But if she was at one of her church meetings and Dad didn't want to cook, off we'd go. He'd have ordered the steak and hash and told us stories about the farm he grew up on out west. We'd have fish and chips and chocolate cake. In the car on the way home he'd prep us.

"What do you say when your mother asks what you ate?"

"Broccoli!" we'd yell in unison, our faces smeared with chocolate.

I arrived early and sat in one of the back booths. I checked the exits and set my phone to ring in fifteen minutes, just in case. The booths had paper placemats with the menus printed on them. The ketchup dispensers looked about a hundred years old. A poster on the wall advertised *The Best Mashed Potatoes in the State!* A pat of butter melting on a mound of mash. Some claim to fame.

Most of the customers looked like truckers. There were a couple of weary-looking moms with their kids. Near the front entrance two teenagers in Slayer shirts were plugging quarters into an ancient arcade game. A girl in tight pink sweatpants stood at one machine, trying to pick up a stuffed animal with a metal claw. The one where the odds are heavily stacked against that ever happening.

"Fucking bullshit," she kept saying, kicking the machine with the toe of her white cowboy boots. More quarters in. The sound of the claw. "Fucking bullshit," again.

I ordered an iced tea with lemon. When I got tired of watching the girl lose her money, I began to thumb through a magazine I'd borrowed from Jackie's bathroom. *Modern Woman's Daily*. I was halfway through "Ten Ways to Keep a Man Happy" when Roger slid onto the bench across from me.

"Hi, Missy," he said quietly. He'd cleaned up, shaved. He was wearing a bright white T-shirt and jeans. He looked even younger, almost humble.

"Hi," I said shyly, immediately wondering why I'd come. What were my reasons? Everything felt so uncertain.

The waitress broke the tension. "Hey, stranger!" she greeted him, placing her hand on his shoulder for a friendly squeeze. "The usual?"

"Thanks, Sam," he said.

She soon returned with a cup of coffee.

He ordered breakfast. When she spoke to me, I could barely find a voice to speak back. I hadn't even thought about eating in all the time I'd been sitting there. I looked at the wall behind Red. "Mashed potatoes," I said, as if possessed by the spirit of some hungry pothead.

She squeezed Red's shoulder again and tousled his hair like he was eight. It occurred to me that she wouldn't likely be so friendly if she'd seen him pointing a gun at a fellow coffee-slinger the day before. He emptied three containers of cream into the small white cup, stirring it slowly with a spoon. Finally he cleared his throat.

"I wanted to apologize."

"Why, why do you want to?" I wasn't going to let him off that easy. What was he really sorry about?

"I'm not a criminal."

"You're in some kind of denial."

"But I'm not."

"You pointed a gun at me. Case in point: criminal. I mean, I don't have a dictionary on me or anything, but I'm pretty sure you fit the definition."

"What I mean is that I have a conscience, right? I would never hurt anyone."

"But you did. You hurt me. You hurt Christina. Just because we don't have holes in our chests doesn't mean you should get a big prize or something."

I moved my hair off my neck and pointed to the bruise. Red looked down at the table. He put his head in his hands. A few seconds passed, and he shifted in his seat.

"This isn't going the way I expected it to go," he said. He looked up, stirred his coffee again. "I thought you wanted to meet me."

"I did. There's something about you. You make me curious."

"Really?"

"Really. I've never met a criminal."

He took a big sip of his coffee. "I'm changing."

"You said that in your note."

The waitress arrived with his plate of scrambled eggs and my mashed potatoes. "But words are just words, right? Actions matter."

"Odd thing to have for breakfast." He nodded in the direction of my plate.

"Apparently they're the best in the state," I said.

"Just an old sign," he said.

They tasted like boxed taters. I dotted them with hot sauce and swirled them around my plate. Cotton candy. I put my fork down and pushed the plate away.

"How are you changing?"

"I want to be someone my daughter can be proud of."

"I understand wanting that. I have a son."

"I've already lost the respect of her brother. He's thirteen now, but he may as well be thirty."

"Thirteen is a crucial age. They still need you, you know."

"With him, it's complicated."

We ate for a few moments in silence. I noticed he ate everything in sections, didn't let the eggs touch the toast or the toast touch the bacon.

"So, why did you rob Callie's?"

"That is also complicated."

"Try me."

* * *

Red proceeded to tell me his whole sorry story. His rocky childhood. His life-changing trip working in the northern woods. How he met his wife. All things I could understand, could picture perfectly. And then the story got stranger, and sadder, and hard to believe.

"So, that's that in a nutshell. You now know more about me than most people in my family."

"Why did you trust me to tell me all that?"

"I'm not sure. Something inside me told me you were special and I could trust you."

"What does *special* mean? That sounds like something women want to hear but means absolutely nothing."

"See? You're tough. You won't let me off the hook for anything, I bet. Just like my ex-wife."

"Yeah, I'm tough," I said. I tried on the world like a sweater. A new style. Sure, Missy Turner, the new version, could be *tough*.

"So, tell your story."

"My story was really boring until yesterday."

"How so?"

"I was happily married for fifteen years."

"Good lord, you look so much younger."

"I got married at seventeen."

"Oh."

"And yesterday I got laid off from my job, came home and found my husband in the arms of the next-door neighbor." I described what had happened. How I'd gasped and dropped the coffee on the floor. Lydia, perfect tits and all, was sitting on Dale's lap, rubbing them in his face. He looked over her shoulder and pushed her off. They both looked at me like scared dogs. She leapt up and ran out the back door.

"Missy! What are you doing here?" Dale had yelped. "Let me explain."

"I'd like to hear you even try."

"Baby, it's not like that."

"I came home because I got laid off today, Dale. And now I find out my husband's a liar? Nice. Great fucking day!" I'd picked up a coffee cup from the counter and threw it at the clock on the wall. They'd both shattered.

I'd turned and run outside. Just in time to see Lydia disappear through her front door.

I got in my car and locked all the doors. I sat perfectly still, tears streaming down my face, while Dale pounded on the hood, yelling variations on "I'm Sorry." Suddenly my world looked different. The sad yard with the drooping begonias. The Rose of Sharon bush that needed trimming. The sagging curtains in the kitchen window that I'd been meaning to fix.

Dale too. With his growing beer gut protruding from his faded Soundgarden Tour T-shirt, his old pair of jogging pants, his slightly receding hairline. He'd finally stopped yelling. Now he was desperately staring into the front window, hands raised in a mock prayer. He'd looked repulsive. I'd started the car and backed out of the driveway. Once in the street, I stopped long enough to open the passenger-side window.

"You fucking disgust me," I'd yelled.

"And he did," I said to Red. "He absolutely disgusted me."

"He sounds like he's not worth your time."

"Well, we've been married fifteen years. It's not like he's some bag of chips I'm done eating."

"Well, you can't *stay* with him."

"You have a pretty good sense of right and wrong for someone who uses guns to make a point."

Red was quiet. For a moment I worried he'd lunge at me. Or get up and leave. But he took a long sip of his coffee and broke into a half smile. "Point taken."

"He wrote me a letter. I haven't even read it yet. I still have it in my purse."

"Read it to me."

For some reason, after Red had just bared his soul to me, I decided, why the hell not.

The letter was terribly written. It over-emphasized how sorry he was. How the thing with Lydia was short-lived and just about sex. We'd been in a rut lately, and he wanted to feel special again. And it was just one time. Lydia wasn't half as beautiful or smart as I was. It was the biggest mistake of his life. How he'd only ever been with me. He'd been so young when we got married. After all these years he was curious about other women. But it hadn't meant anything. I'm the only thing that meant anything. Blah, blah, blah... Three pages essentially saying the same thing over and over.

"What I don't understand is that if he was so curious about other women and wanted to experiment, why be so uncreative and choose the tramp next door?"

Red smiled. "Men are essentially assholes. And lazy."

"Whatever. That's just an excuse. How can all of one group be the same way? Women certainly can't agree on much."

"Yeah, but there's something to the idea that men will try to get away with what they can…sometimes. But some of us can change. I'm trying. You're my inspiration."

"You just met me. That's such a line."

"It's the god's honest truth."

"Well, at least I'm something to someone, right?" Until I formed those words, I had no idea how lonely I felt.

I pictured Dale on the days he'd make me dinner—lasagna, meatloaf or vaguely awkward pad thai. He'd rub my shoulders after he placed the plate in front of me, smiling like he should be given a medal for cooking a meal. There was something endearing about him, and infuriating at the same time. I missed him so much at that moment I could hardly speak.

Sam arrived to ask if we'd like the bill.

"I'll have a beer and a shot of whiskey," I said.

Red looked surprised. "Sounds like a good plan."

CHAPTER EIGHT

At one o'clock, we were still sitting in the diner. The better part of a pitcher of watery beer sat between us. I suppose it had something to do with the way we met, but neither of us were shy. We laid it out on the table, so to speak.

"I just don't know what to do with my life now," I said. "I don't feel like I can just go back. Too much has changed."

"I know I can't. I just want to make a new life for myself." Red appeared energized by the new possibilities.

"If only it were easy to make big changes. There's a part of me that wants to go back to Dale and our house. And just wait for Mike to come home next month. Pretend nothing happened at all. It's the only thing I know. It's so comfortable, right?"

Roger shrugged. "Nothing has felt comfortable for a long time."

"Where could I go?" I felt like spinning a globe and pointing down anywhere, the way they do in adventure stories. "I could take a trip. By myself."

"I have a brother in New York City," he said. "We could take a trip together. Stay with him for a few days. You could rest, get some perspective."

I looked into the bottom of my pint glass and felt dizzy. Suddenly I was free as a bird, at least for six weeks. No job, my son away. A husband I couldn't bear to look at. I could be anyone. I had a savings account. I'd been squirreling away funds for an emergency for the past eight years. Maybe this was one.

I could be the girl who bolts into the bathroom and throws up from the shock and sorrow. Then she gets in her car and goes and cries on her largely unsympathetic sister's shoulder. Or I could be the girl who suggests getting a room at the Motel 6 across the road. Because the relatively dangerous man across from her makes her feel like a lit match. I could be that girl, the girl I've always been in awe of in movies. In the moment and unafraid.

CHAPTER NINE

As we lay back against bleached white sheets, breathing in the odor of sickening strawberry deodorant and smoke-soaked carpeting, it occurred to me that maybe my husband had a point. I laughed out loud when I thought this. The cackle of my laughter jarred Red, who'd been lying next to me, staring at the ceiling. Maybe there is something to having sex with someone you haven't known since you were a Clearasil-smeared prom date.

The cliché is true—that the line between humor and tragedy is so thin sometimes.

"What's so funny?" Roger asked, smiling sideways at me.

"Nothing," I said.

"What?"

"You know, I've never done that before."

"Oh, c'mon, you've definitely done *that* before."

"No, jerk. I mean, I've only ever had sex with my husband. I was a virgin before him."

"Really?"

"We got married so young."

"Huh."

"I bet you've had tons of ladies."

Red smiled and shrugged. "Well, more than one."

We lit cigarettes like we were in some 1970s movie. Lying side by side, staring at the ceiling.

"So, you want to come with me to the city?" he asked. "New York City, imagine that."

I snuggled up to him, laid my head on his chest. "I just might. How is it you can leave your kid like that?"

"She's with my mother this week. They think I'm off working for the week, but the truth is I got fired."

"Why'd you get fired?"

"Long story." I felt a twinge in my gut about him lying to his mother. Then I thought, Well, who doesn't lie to his mother on occasion? My mother certainly didn't know everything about me.

"Well, I've clearly got all the time I need to hear it."

"One of my managers was out to get me. I was late a few times. Enough said."

"How come you didn't tell your mom?"

"She thinks I can't do anything right. It kills me that, since all this bad shit went down, she has to help out. I need her and I never wanted to need her again. I don't want Trisha around her, but I have no other choice. It's not like I can afford day care."

"So, what are you going to do?"

"Run away with a beautiful girl, maybe? Figure something out in the city? My brother's got a good job. He can probably help me out." Red looked at the ceiling when he said that, and closed his eyes.

"In the meantime, let's just stay here for the night. We've already paid up after all. Let's have some fun, relax, pretend we're teenagers!"

"Sounds like a good idea…"

"I'll go get some ice," I said, "for the beer."

Red got up and went to the bathroom. I pocketed my driver's license and twenty bucks, and purposely left my purse on the bed. The red leather clutch open invitingly. I took a long time getting the ice. I stopped at the convenience store across the street to get a bottle of vodka, some soda water and a few bags of chips. I stared so long at the gum, the cashier started to look uncomfortable.

"Don't worry, I'm not going to steal anything!" I said, my voice going up in pitch with each word. "I'm just feeling indecisive."

The cashier looked unimpressed. I put two strips of grape licorice on the counter with my drinks and snacks. I had the purchasing habits of a teenager, but I didn't care. After all, I never really got to finish being a teenager.

I walked slowly down the hotel hallway, hands creased with the red circles from the imprint of the plastic bags. I was half expecting Red might have vanished with my purse and car. My instincts felt right—that I could generally trust him. But still, he had held a gun to my throat a mere twenty-four hours ago. I might be having a little circumstantial nervous breakdown, but I could still be cautious.

He was lying on the bed, shirtless, watching TV.

"I can't believe how cool Gene Simmons used to be and what he's become now." Gene was toddling around a mansion on the screen. My purse was in the same position I left it.

I handed him a whip of licorice. He looked at it oddly, before popping it in his mouth. "You eat like you're eight."

"No more whole grains for me. I'm all about the flavor!" I had no idea what I was talking about. Red grinned.

I decided to take a shower. While the water poured into the empty stall, I sat on the counter beside the sink and called Jackie. I left a message. I'd gone out of town to think, I said. Not to worry. I'd be back soon enough. I asked her to feed Simon or remind Dale to. To stop by the house and make sure Lydia wasn't over. Generally make Dale crazy. I asked her not to call unless it was an emergency. I tried to sound mysterious, like I was on some sort of mission.

When I emerged from the steam, I walked back into the hotel room where Red was now sleeping to the sounds of MTV's *Countdown*. It was five o'clock. Dale would be getting up for work about now. His last text read, *I love you so much. I always will. Don't doubt that.*

* * *

It was midnight when Red got out of bed. Our bodies had been getting acquainted for nearly twelve hours. He opened the sliding glass door and stood on the balcony, smoking. When he came back into the room, he looked energized, hyper.

"Let's go now! I love driving at night! There's a full moon too." He jumped onto the bed, on his knees.

"Are you drunk? Are you sure you can drive?"

"No, I had my last drink hours ago."

I noticed his half-full beer still on the nightstand.

"Are you sure? I paid for the whole night already." He seemed to almost bristle at the mention that I'd paid for the room. This should have been a warning.

"But we can be on the ROAD! We can start the adventure now." He was like a kid talking about taking a unicorn ride to Mars Bar Mountain. It was infectious. When was the last time I'd been on the road at night, or ever really? The air outside was still warm, a perfect summer breeze. I felt like an outlaw. It would be fitting to travel at night. After all, we'd spent the whole day inside.

"You trust me, right?" he said, stubbing his cigarette out in the ashtray.

"I suppose I'm starting to."

"I promise, I'll give you every reason to. The way we met, it will be the only mistake I ever make with you. I'm a good man, Missy. I promise you I am."

His eyes were wide-open, and I felt like I had the keys to a new world. I was happy to explore it. Cautious living had only got me so far. Time to try a new tactic.

CHAPTER TEN

We stood next to our two cars in the parking lot.

"Which one should we take?" I asked. "Mine's pretty good on gas."

For some reason, it felt like a good idea to be in my own car. Safe. If this were a movie, we'd have jumped into some shiny convertible and been off without another thought. In real life, there were details.

"I don't know. Mine is roomier. And we can always come back and get your car later. You can park it in the restaurant's parking lot. Sam will make sure it doesn't get towed."

"Sam's probably not still on shift."

"I'll call her."

He started pushing buttons on his phone, mind already made up.

"Do you live around here or something? How do you know this place so well?"

"Yeah, my place is just a few miles east, on Concession Road 8. I used to work in the gas station as a teenager. Sam's a friend of the family."

We drove the cars across the street. I parked in a spot marked *Employees Only*. Red went into the gas station and emerged with a sign to put on the dashboard of my car. And a box of donuts.

For the first two hours we talked non-stop. About our adolescence. Who we wanted to be as adults. Faces smeared with jelly filling.

"I suppose that when I met Andrea, I thought our life was just beginning. It was total happiness for four straight years.

I came home from work excited. It was like I was going to meet my favorite celebrity every single night. That's how excited she made me."

It's funny, but at that moment I almost felt jealous of a dead woman. Still, I could relate. I used to feel that way about Dale. I tried to push Dale out of my mind. I looked out the window at the rows of cornfields. The full moon lighting up the sky. Red drove just a little over the speed limit, but very safely. For some reason I'd pegged him as an erratic speeder. I normally don't relax when other people drive. Jackie says it's because I'm controlling.

"Some days I still wake up calling for her."

What if I'd walked into the kitchen yesterday and found Dale dead instead of cheating? I couldn't even imagine how that would feel.

And that's what happened to Red. He walked in and found his beloved shot.

She was slumped over the kitchen table where she'd been eating her breakfast. Shot by her ex-husband. But Red didn't know that at first. She was just shot.

It was a terrible story. Her ex had just been released from prison. He'd spent thirteen years inside for beating her up. She had been pregnant at the time. A neighbor had heard her screams and called 9-1-1. Her ex then assaulted one of the cops with a baseball bat. He went away for fifteen years. Unfortunately when he was paroled, no one warned his ex-wife. She'd moved many times and had taken Red's last name. As a result the authorities couldn't find her. But he could.

Red had been at work at the time of the shooting. He drove combine for a farmer a few miles outside of town and was working alone. There was no one to confirm his story. The investigating officers maintained that he had enough time to do the shooting and return to work.

When he got home and found his wife dead, Red collapsed over her body, sobbing. Moments later his twelve-year-old stepson arrived home from school. He walked into the kitchen and saw them both covered in blood. Panicked, he ran to the neighbor's house. The housewife, who babysat his little sister, still only a toddler, called the cops.

When the cops arrived, no matter how many times he said, "I found her, I found her," they were skeptical. Who else would want to kill her? The fact that his son wouldn't speak—couldn't speak for weeks—didn't help anything.

For lack of any other suspects—and a string of earlier assault charges for bar fights, the cops charged Red. He didn't have money for a good lawyer. He lost his job and all his savings in legal fees. He spent four months in jail. They'd had no life insurance. For four agonizing months, his kids went to his mom. When the police finally figured out who the real killer was, Red was broke...and broken.

"Jail hardened me," he said as we drove through the night. "Even though it was only four months. I feel like the old me, he's just not around anymore. I miss being him. And it really feels like everyone is always out to get me. I can't catch a break."

"Maybe your luck is changing." I smiled. I took his right hand off the wheel and placed it on my breast. He smiled.

Just before dawn I drifted to sleep in the front seat. Red's hand on my leg, smiling at each other like we'd been together for years. There was something so comforting in his face and the way he touched me. The way he looked more interested in me than Dale ever had been.

I woke up when the car stopped in front of some gas pumps. There was a pink band of light on the horizon.

"Are we out of gas?" I asked, like an idiot.

I stretched my arms and unclipped my seatbelt.

"Yeah."

"I'll get this one," I said, pulling out my wallet. I didn't want him to feel bad about not having money.

"Missy, it's okay. The money I stole went to buy my daughter her asthma medication. I've got enough for gas, right?"

I knew it wasn't true. I'd looked in his wallet when he was in the shower. Ten bucks and a thirty-days-sober chip from AA.

"Please, Roger. Let me pay this time. I have some money saved up."

Roger looked down, before opening the car door.

"Whatever," he said gruffly.

I got out of the car and walked around to where he was starting to fill up. I handed him forty dollars. I held his free hand in mine and kissed him on the mouth. He was still tense but seemed to relax a little.

"I'm going to the bathroom," I announced, hoping to get the imprint of the seatbelt off my face.

"Okay." He shrugged. His eyes had a faraway look.

Standing at the long row of sinks, I pressed some concealer under my eyes. I turned on my cell phone. A text from Jackie: *Where the hell are you? Dale and I are worried sick.* When was the last night I stayed out until dawn? Probably grade ten.

I wondered if eventually I could make up a story about how I met Red. How I took an impromptu trip to the city and met him at a restaurant. How we'd eaten at the counter next to each other. It was love at first sight. No one would have to know.

I looked in the mirror and turned around, looking at myself from a few different angles. I was suddenly dizzy at the memory of our last kiss. It made me breathless just thinking about it. I actually had butterflies in my stomach. I couldn't stop grinning at myself in the mirror, smoothing out my lips with a sparkled gloss.

I pushed open the door and walked into the food court. There was a small crowd of early morning commuters, truckers, long-distance travelers. All seemed to be drinking absurdly large cups of coffee. As I walked, I felt like the world was my own catwalk. I was actually strutting. In a service station, wearing a slept-in dress, no less. But it didn't matter. This was me now, a traveler, an adventuress, newly in love.

I stopped at a display of gumball and toy machines that lined the hall between the bathrooms and the fast-food counters. Each machine had different toys or candy to choose from, housed in clear plastic eggs. I picked out a small dog figurine meant for a car dashboard. Its head bobbed up and down. It could be Red's good-luck dog, I reasoned. I chose the pit bull.

The cold plastic globe felt good in my hands.

And that was the last good feeling I had that day.

I felt it first. A sudden quiet, the shuffling of shoes on the concrete floor, nervous movement. I walked toward the food court, peering around the corner at the Wendy's counter. Red had his back to me. From the expression on the young cashier's face, I knew what he was doing. I ducked down behind a garbage can, leveled by shock. I pulled out my phone, dialing 9-1-1. The trouble was I didn't really know where we were. I whispered vague possibilities, hoping someone who'd made it outside had also called.

"Stop running or I will shoot! Get down on the ground, everyone!" Roger's voice was different now, more forceful. No more niceties like at Callie's. When he said he would shoot, this time I believed him. But he still hadn't seen me. Does he think I'm just waiting in the car for him like an idiot? If I stood up, I'd be an accomplice. If I stood up, he could shoot me. Who was this man I'd just spent the better part of two days with? The one I was fantasizing about marrying? Did losing everything in one fell swoop mean I'd also lost my mind? Any semblance of intelligence and character?

I was only a few feet from the door. I thought about making a run for it. Then a middle-aged man beat me to it, and Roger actually shot at him. The bullet hit the glass door. It shattered. He missed the man, who kept running. People on the floor were whimpering. The cashier was sobbing. Roger himself looked quite shocked at what he'd done.

"Please, mister, just take the money from the till."

"I want all of it. Everything from the safe."

"I don't know the code! Only the manager does! He's not here."

"Bullshit!"

"Seriously, I would give it to you if I could. You think I want to die for this stupid job? I don't care! I'd rather live!"

"I will shoot you, girl, I swear."

"I will call him. Let me call him."

That's when I stood up. Mostly because at that moment I felt a responsibility for our being there. I felt like if that girl got shot, it would be partially on me.

"Roger, put the gun down."

He turned to me. "Shut up. Get to the car, keep it running."

"Look at her, she's just a girl. She's just a little older than Trisha."

"Shut up, Missy. I mean it."

He didn't look flustered or shaken like he did at Callie's. He was not some kid making a mistake. Right then, he looked like he'd done this kind of thing a million times. He looked like he thought he deserved that money.

"What about our plan? Getting to the city? Your brother helping us out? Why do you need to do this?"

"Shut up, Missy. I mean it."

"Just take what you have and go. Leave me here."

He seemed to be considering it. Sweat dripped onto his forehead. The girl behind the counter looked at me, pleading.

"I'm not leaving without you," he said, in a way that sounded like he'd stuff me in a paper sac if he had to.

"I'm not going anywhere with you, you fucking liar."

Incredibly, Roger had the balls to look *hurt* by what I said.

"Sweetheart," I said to the cashier, "just get down on the floor, okay? He's not going to hurt you."

Roger looked at me. "I'm in charge here, Missy, not you!"

"You don't want to hurt her. Remember, you're a good man. Remember saying that? She's just a young girl. Take the gun off of her."

He backed up and put the gun down slightly, before turning and aiming it at me.

"Is this what you want then?" he said, like a petulant child.

"Better me than her," I said. I raised my hands.

"Oh, Missy, such a hero."

"What about all the stuff you said, about me making you change, giving us a chance at something new? What about your brother?"

"I don't even have a brother. I'm just making this up as we go. I just wanted us to leave and start a new life. And now you're fucking it all up. I had a plan, Missy. See what I mean? Someone always fucks it up. I had it settled until you interrupted."

We heard the sirens first. Then flashing red and blue lights filled the parking lot.

"What about Andrea? What if she's watching you right now?"

"She's dead, Missy. It doesn't matter anymore. Plus, she was no saint. She would be in the car right now, keeping the engine running."

So that's what they were. They worked together. He missed his accomplice.

"Give me the gun."

"No."

"Let people go. Let the women go, at least, the kids. C'mon."

He stayed silent.

"Keep the gun on me, and let everyone go."

He nodded. "Okay, everyone walk out slowly!" he yelled, as if it was his idea. Slowly, people started getting up, unsure if they were making the right decision. A few brave ones lifted their arms and started running toward the door. They filed out. The whole time, Red's eyes were locked on mine.

"Baby, you said you believed in me, trusted me..."

Then two cops barged in the door.

He still had the gun on me.

"Put down your weapon, we can work this out," said the first cop.

"Don't hurt me, please," came out of my mouth, weakly. Red shook his head back and forth.

"Put down the weapon or we will have to shoot," the other cop said. "It's over."

I watched Roger look at me for a long second, his eyes black marbles of nothingness. Then he slowly lowered the gun to his side. Both cops ran toward him. Just as they reached him, he raised the gun and pulled the trigger.

* * *

I woke up on a stretcher. Someone was yelling at me…a paramedic.

"What's your name?" he kept yelling. I tried to answer his question.

"What happened? What happened?" I asked.

"You were shot," the young man said. "In the arm. You're going to be okay. But you hit your head when you fell. Just hang in there."

"What happened to the man who shot me?"

"They've arrested him."

Then everything went white. I could still hear a roaring sound and the clicking of instruments. I grabbed someone's hand and held on.

I woke up in the hospital. Beside my bed stood a very curious lady cop who had a lot of questions for me.

EPILOGUE

It's the day before Mike comes home. Dale is finishing some touch-ups on the back deck. The reporters have stopped hounding me, and my arm has healed. I'm lying on a deck chair on the grass out back. Simon is snuggled at my feet, washing his face with a curled paw. Dale works silently, every once in a while glancing up to smile.

I'm leafing through Mike's last letter home. He's fallen in love with a girl named Lisa, who likes to ride BMX bikes and lives a hundred miles away.

Next door, Lydia's soon-to-be-ex husband and his new girlfriend wave, and then continue to covertly whisper about me behind the barbeque.

The rumors of my crazy breakdown—running off with a criminal and getting arrested—do not seem to have lost their appeal to anyone yet. My sister's been great as a supporter. My parents, though, are still struggling to understand what happened. In all honesty, so am I. Dale's been staying with his parents for most of the summer, but he slept over last night. We're trying to work things out. And figure out what to tell Michael in the meantime. We want to make sure he's prepared to go to school, with what must be going around. It's actually kind of a relief to not have to talk about us for a change. Just focus on our kid's happiness, something much less complicated than adult happiness.

In a few months there will be a court date for Red, and I have to testify against him. Of course, I confessed to everything. My lawyer argued that I'd been unwilling to see myself as a victim when Red held up the café. That I'd suffered some version of the Stockholm syndrome. They let me off with probation, community service and mandatory counseling.

The weirdest thing is, sometimes I think about Red in prison and I feel bad. After everything he did, I still feel some compassion. Like he's some one-eyed kitten who can't stop hurting himself. I know this is crazy. I'm still absorbing it all. I think I've still got a ways to go. The truth is, I never knew him at all. My therapist suggests he's not knowable. I think she's probably right. It was my therapist who suggested I write everything down. Every moment I didn't understand. Try to lay it all out in front of me. Try to make sense of it all. Some day maybe.

It's fitting, I suppose, that Mike is on his way home. And I'm slowly starting to trust Dale again. The days are getting shorter. I feel like I'm almost back in the middle of a normal life. And I've reached the end of this notebook.

ZOE WHITTALL is the author of five books, most recently the critically acclaimed *Holding Still For As Long As Possible* and *Bottle Rocket Hearts*, a *Globe and Mail* Best Book of 2007. She has a master's degree from the University of Guelph. Originally from Quebec, she has lived in Toronto since 1997.

978-1-55469-262-0 $9.95 pb

Someone is killing some of Charlie D's
favorite listeners.

Charlie D is the host of a successful late-night radio
call-in show. His listeners have a particularly intimate
relationship with him and often reveal much about
themselves, confident that he will honor their trust and
that he can save them. In their minds, he is perfect:
one of life's winners. But Charlie feels he's something
of a fake. His easy confidence on-air belies the reality
for a man born with a wine-colored birthmark that
covers half his face.

Love You to Death covers one hour on "The World
According to Charlie D"—an hour during which he
must both discover the long-time listener who is killing
the people who trust him and attempt to come to terms
with the man behind the birthmark.

978-1-55469-282-8 $9.95 pb

"My name is Rick Montoya. But you can call me the Spider. Other people do."

When detective Rick Montoya returns to the city to try to clear his name after being accused of taking a bribe, he discovers someone is living in his apartment. Before he can find out who it is, the apartment house goes up in flames. Rick watches covertly as the police remove two bodies. Was the firebombing meant for him? Who exactly was killed in the fire? And why? What was his landlady Cheryl doing at home in the middle of the afternoon? And why is her daughter Susanna acting strangely? Then his estranged wife arrives at the scene of the fire. The questions mount up, along with the suspects.